Cinderella

Retold by Susanna Davidson

Illustrated by
Fabiano Fiorin

Reading Consultant: Alison Kelly
Roehampton University

Contents

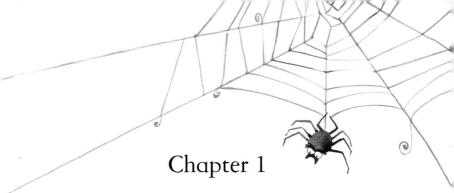

Chapter 1

Invitation to a ball

"Cinderella!" shouted her stepmother, looking up from a letter. "Come and clean my bedroom at once."

3

"Yes, Stepmother," Cinderella called from the kitchen, where she was making lunch. Her stepsisters had ordered their usual revolting dishes.

Urgh!

"Well, I've made the sausage trifle," Cinderella thought to herself. "The cabbage and custard pie will just have to wait."

She picked up her broom and made her way to the stairs. But her stepsisters were blocking the way.

"What's little Cinders doing today then?" teased Griselda.

"She's sweeping away cobwebs, like a servant," sneered Grimella.

5

"Get on with it then,
servant girl," said Griselda.
Just then, Cinderella's
stepmother appeared.

"Griselda, Grimella," she cried.
"I have the most exciting news.
The Prince is giving a Christmas
Ball and you're invited."

"We'll dress you in the finest clothes – only the best for my beautiful darlings. Isn't that right, dear?" she said to Cinderella's father.

Cinderella gripped her broom hard. "May I go to the Ball as well?" she asked, in a scared whisper.

"You? Go to the Ball?" said her stepmother. "You must be joking. You belong in the kitchen."

Cinderella turned to her father, but he coughed and looked away. "He's too scared of Stepmother to help me," thought Cinderella. "If only I could go to the Ball..."

Chapter 2

A surprise visit

"We'll be the most beautiful girls there," chorused the stepsisters.

"I'm sure the Prince will want to marry one of you," said their mother, proudly.

"Now, Cinderella," she went on, "as a special treat and since it's nearly Christmas…"

"Yes?" Cinderella cried.

"You may help Griselda and Grimella choose their dresses."

All that week, boot-makers, dressmakers, wig-makers and hairdressers streamed through the door.

Cinderella tried to make
her stepsisters look as pretty
as possible. It wasn't easy.

Grimella wanted to wear a
hat decorated with stuffed birds.
Griselda chose a lime green dress
with yellow spots.

"What about feathers, rather than stuffed birds, Grimella?" Cinderella suggested politely. "And Griselda, I think the yellow dress suited you better."

Shut up, Cinders!

"What would you know?" said Grimella. "But you might be right. We must look grander than everyone else. Sew on lots of rubies and ribbons."

Cinderella worked all day and all night, putting the finishing touches to their outfits.

Hurry up, Cinderella.

At last they were ready. Cinderella's stepsisters gazed at themselves in the mirror.

"Don't we look gorgeous!" they shrieked. "We'll be the finest ladies at the Ball."

"Oh my Tinkerbells, you look wonderful," their mother gasped. "Let's go! The coach is here. Cinderella – put up the Christmas decorations while we're gone."

The front door was opened. There was a swish of skirts and a blast of cold air. Then Cinderella was left alone.

As she struggled with the Christmas tree, tears blurred her eyes. "Oh!" she sobbed, getting tangled in tinsel. "I wish – I *wish* I could go to the Ball."

A loud crash in the chimney made Cinderella look up. There, in the fireplace, covered in soot, was her godmother.

15

Chapter 3

Fantastic Felicity

"Godmother Felicity," cried
Cinderella, "whatever are you
doing in our chimney?"

"I missed the door," Felicity
replied airily.

"But I haven't seen you since I was ten," said Cinderella.

"I've been with Sleeping Beauty, my other godchild," explained Felicity. "But she wouldn't wake up, so it was rather dull."

"Have you been crying, Cinders?" asked Felicity, looking at her closely.

"Yes! I wanted to go to the Ball, but I'm not allowed."

"Well, you can wipe those tears away, girlie. Fantastic Felicity is here to help. Now, go to the garden and fetch me a large pumpkin."

"Great," thought Cinderella, "my stepsisters are at the Ball and I'm picking up pumpkins for my crazy godmother."

"Here you are," Cinderella said, a few minutes later. "It's the biggest one."

"Jolly good," Felicity replied. "This shouldn't take long."

Now... what was the spell?

"Um, Felicity..." said Cinderella.

"Yes dear?" said Felicity.

"Why are you waving that stick around?"

19

"This isn't a stick, Cinderella," her godmother replied. "It's a wand. The time has come to tell you a great secret. Your godmother is a fairy!"

Really?

"Watch!" she went on. Felicity flicked her wand at the pumpkin and cried out, "Abracadabra, cadabra cadeen!"

Cinderella waited. Nothing happened. "I don't know much about fairies," Cinderella said, "but shouldn't you be using the other end of your wand?"

Well spotted, Cinderella!

"Silly me!" said Felicity. "Soot on the brain. Let's try again."

There was a wonderful tinkle of music and a shower of sparks. In the place of the pumpkin stood a beautiful golden coach.

Cinderella gasped. "You really can do magic!"

"Yes," said Felicity, "and this is just the beginning. Now, where's your mousetrap?"

"Under the sink," said Cinderella. Felicity peered in.

"Six mice, one fat rat, all alive. Excellent. Open the mousetrap door, Cinderella."

Kazaam!

As each of the mice came out, Felicity gave them a little tap with her wand.

One by one, the mice were transformed into fine white horses. The rat became a rosy-cheeked coachman, with very large whiskers.

"Now I need six lizards," said Felicity. "Hmm... I expect there'll be some behind your watering can."

"There are!" said Cinderella, handing them to her godmother. In a flash, the lizards became footmen.

At your s-s-s-service, Cinderella.

They were dressed in glistening green and looked as if they'd been footmen all their lives.

"There you are, Cinderella," said Felicity, sounding rather pleased with herself. "Now you can go to the Ball."

I'll be off now.

"But I can't go in these rags!" Cinderella cried out.

Felicity touched Cinderella
with her wand. A moment
later, her rags turned into
a dazzling dress of gold
and silver.

On her feet
was a perfect pair
of little glass slippers.

27

"There's just one problem,"
said Felicity. "You must leave
before twelve. On the last
stroke of midnight, my magic
will begin to fade."

"I promise," Cinderella
replied, climbing into the
coach. "And thank you so
much!" she called, as the
horses swept her away.

Chapter 4

At the Ball

When Cinderella entered the ballroom, everyone fell silent. Then slowly, a whisper went around the room.

Who can she be?

"Who's that beautiful girl?" the ladies wondered. "She must be a princess."

A voice next to Cinderella almost made her jump. It was the Prince. "May I have this dance?" he asked.

Cinderella and the Prince twirled across the floor. "She's so graceful," said the other ladies. "And look at her dress! Have you ever seen anything so delicate?"

Ignore her!

"The Prince is only being polite," said Grimella. "He'd much rather dance with me."

Cinderella was enjoying herself so much, she forgot to watch the time. As the Prince whirled her around the room, she caught sight of the clock.

The time!

"Oh no!" she said. "It's almost midnight. I must go."

Cinderella pulled away from the Prince and ran across the dance floor. The Prince raced after her. "Come back," he called.

I don't even know your name.

But Cinderella had disappeared into the darkness.

"Have you seen a girl in a gold and silver dress?" the Prince asked the palace guard.

"No," said the guard. "A girl ran past a moment ago, but she was dressed in rags."

I've lost her.

The Prince turned back to the palace with a sigh. Then something on the steps caught his eye. "Her glass slipper!" he cried.

34

Chapter 5

The glass slipper

Cinderella ran
home as fast as
she could. She arrived
just before her stepsisters.

"How was the Ball?" Cinderella asked.

"It was very grand," said Griselda. "Far too grand for the likes of you."

I'm sure the Prince is in love with me.

Cinderella smiled, but she said nothing.

36

The next morning, the entire
street was woken by the shout
of a town crier, who was
followed by a messenger.

By the order of his
royal highness, the
Prince, every girl in the
kingdom must try on this
glass slipper. The
Prince will marry its
true owner.

Cinderella's stepmother flung open the front door and grabbed the messenger.

"One of my girls will fit this shoe," she said proudly, "and then I'll be queen."

Griselda couldn't even fit her big toe in the shoe. She pushed until her foot was bright red.

"Give it to me!" shouted Grimella, and snatched the glass slipper from her sister. Grimella rammed half her foot in the shoe, but then it got stuck.

"Squeeze, Grimella," shrieked her mother. "You're not trying hard enough."

"I'm trying as hard as I can, Mama," said Grimella, with a grunt.

Ow!

"You useless child," cried her mother. She wrenched the slipper off Grimella's foot and flung it at the messenger. "Off you go then," she snapped.

The messenger cleared his throat. "Excuse me, ma'am," he said, "but my strict orders are that every young lady is to try on the shoe." He looked directly at Cinderella.

What about this girl?

"What?" said Grimella. "She's just a servant. You needn't bother with her."

Cinderella's father coughed. "Actually..." he began.

"Shut up you stupid man," interrupted the stepmother.

"...Cinderella has as much right to try on the slipper as anyone," he went on, bravely.

"Oh Papa!" said Cinderella. She walked over to the messenger and slipped on the shoe. It was a perfect fit.

"No!" shrieked Griselda
and Grimella.

"She can't be a princess,"
shouted their mother. "I won't
allow it."

This is all
your fault.

"Get out!" she screamed at
the messenger. "I want you to
pretend this never happened."

With one swift movement,
the messenger swept off his hat
and cloak. Everyone in the
room gasped. It was the Prince.

You!

He strode over to Cinderella.
"I would have searched my
kingdom for you," he said.
"Will you marry me?"

Cinderella smiled. "Oh yes!" she replied.

At that moment, there was a puff of smoke and Felicity flew into the room.

She held her wand above her head and a starry mist swirled around them all. "Time for a little more magic," she declared.

Felicity flicked her wand
and gave Cinderella a dress
even more beautiful than the
one she had worn to the Ball.

Thank you!

"My princess!" said the
Prince, and swept Cinderella
off to his palace. Cinderella
and the Prince were married
the very next day...

...and lived happily ever after. Griselda and Grimella were not so happy.

We wanted to marry the Prince.

Their mother never stopped scolding them. "It's all your fault for having such big feet," she told them.

There are over 700 versions of Cinderella.
Cinderella has also been known as Rashin Coatie
in Scotland, Aschenputtel in Germany, Zezolla in
Italy, and Yeh-hsien in China. This version is from
a retelling by Charles Perrault, a French writer
who lived in the seventeenth century.

Series editor: Lesley Sims
Designed by Russell Punter
and Katarina Dragoslavic

First published in 2004 by Usborne Publishing Ltd., Usborne House,
83-85 Saffron Hill, London EC1N 8RT, England. www.usborne.com
Copyright © 2004 Usborne Publishing Ltd.